I0763556

Compatible Strangers

Danni Peters

Compatible Strangers

A Divine Destiny

Danni Peters

Published by Felicity Fox Books Publishing House

www.thefelicityfoxhouse.com

Identifiers:

Canada © 1194342

ISBN: 978-1-7782441-0-0 (hardback)

ISBN: 978-1-7782441-1-7 (ebook)

Available in hardback and ebook.

https://www.facebook.com/petersdanni

Interior Design and Editing by: Felicity Fox

Cover design by: Cosmic Letterz

Contents

One

The cold darkness of the night had closed in on her. After each blinding flash of light, thunder crashed loudly, and rain fell in a continuous cascade penetrating her fur. The drenched and terrified golden Labrador retriever and Pitbull mix dog was exhausted, lonely, and hungry. She was no longer sure how long she had been left behind on the long barren stretch of road and tried her best to stay under a fallen tree for protection. It did nothing to keep the rain, thunder, and snapping lightning sounds away, but it offered enough leaves to block the blinding light flashes. Not sure how long she laid there, she eventually felt the storm subside to a drizzle. Finally, she gathered herself up and looked across the landscape.

She could make out the outline of the highway in the distance as it weaved a wavy trail down the hillside. When she tried to get up, her energy was too depleted, and her body fought her efforts. She blinked her tired eyes and thought about going to sleep, but instead, she kept them open and noticed a bright light in the clouds. Intrigued, she stood up. Even though the sky was dark with rain clouds, the light began to beam down and hover over the highway. At the same time, she noticed the beige PT Cruiser driving toward her.

"Get to that car."

She heard the whispered words and felt a surge of energy course through her body, so she ran out into the highway to meet the car.

Aaron Peterik was late leaving for work that day. As he sped down the winding highway, the rain steadily fell amid lightning flashes and thunder roars, yet he continued toward the small town of Victory. The storm seemed to subside as Aaron reached the mountain's summit. He applied the brakes gently and began the descent into the valley below because he had made this drive to town daily for the last five years and knew the stretch of highway like the back of his hand. Deer and moose almost constantly crossed the road in the valley, so he knew to slow down on this particular stretch.

"What is that?" mused Aaron out loud.

A bright light appeared briefly in the road ahead, lasting only a moment. Then, Aaron could make out the form of a soaking wet dog standing in the middle of the road. He immediately hit the brakes and screeched to a halt.

"Oh, please God, no!" he prayed. "Please let the poor dog be okay."

He jumped out of his car to assess the situation. *Oh, thank God,* Aaron thought when he saw the dog still standing on the road, approximately two feet in front of his car, but the poor thing was a sorry sight to behold. Nevertheless, Aaron felt her plea for help deep within his being.

"Hey there, friend," said Aaron. "What are you doing out here?"

He slowly approached the dog, but the dog backed up a step as a memory flashed in its mind of a mean man hitting her with a long-jagged stick. Instinctively, she growled and showed her teeth. Aaron stopped and contemplated the situation. Though he didn't see any sign of human activity, it was impossible to see any fresh tracks along the road with the heavy rainfall. He cautiously moved toward his car and opened the passenger door.

"C'mon, dog, get inside and warm up," he said.

The dog stopped growling and turned her head to one side, her ears perked up, and her big brown eyes opened wide. Then she jumped into Aaron's car. He watched her sit down as he closed the door. Then, she stood back up and shook the water out of her fur. The drops of dirt and water splashed inside the car, landing on the windows, seats, and dash.

Aaron laughed aloud. "That's it. Make yourself comfortable, my friend."

He got back into the car and started driving toward the town. The dog had curled up in the seat beside him and was already dozing off. From time to time, however, she slowly opened one eye and looked at him.

Aaron decided to follow his regular normal routine as they approached the town. He pulled into the local coffee shop drive-thru and ordered his coffee and lunch, then added a breakfast sandwich with extra meat to his order. When they got to the window, the enticing smell of fresh baked goods permeated the car, waking the dog. Aaron chuckled when the dog sat up and asked the lady in the window to add a fresh plain donut to the order.

"That is a big order for you this morning, Aaron." She chuckled. "Did you forget to have dinner last night?"

"No, Carol, I seemed to have picked up a new friend on the way to work. Furthermore, she looks hungry." Aaron responded with a smile as he leaned back to show off the dog.

Because Aaron stopped daily for his coffee and breakfast, he and Carol always engaged in friendly banter. He told her about finding and rescuing the dog and asked if she had heard of anyone losing or looking for a dog, but she hadn't and offered to ask around.

He collected his order and drove to his office, the dog showing great interest in the breakfast bag . When they arrived in the parking lot, Aaron grabbed the bag, an old blanket from the trunk, and opened the door for the dog. She jumped out and followed him inside.

Two

Though the rain had subsided, the morning was gloomy and dark with a weird, gray, cloud-covered, intimidating sky. Aaron was tall with a lean, muscular build. Even though he had a triple black belt in martial arts, he had a meek and reserved persona and carried himself with quiet confidence. A bail bondsman by trade, Aaron went about his business at his oversized wooden desk, calling clients and filing the necessary documents. Occasionally, clients came in seeking help for their predicaments; otherwise, he worked alone.

The dog, whom he affectionately called Gurlz, slept under Aaron's desk on her blanket. She immediately gobbled up all he had offered to her that morning, including his lunch, and seemed to enjoy the cozy warm atmosphere. She could not remember ever feeling this secure in her life. Nevertheless, she awoke to Aaron's gentle voice calling her.

"Gurlz, come on, Gurlz. It is lunchtime," he said with a laugh. "We shall have to venture out and get more."

He reached down and patted her on the head. She stretched out her body and got up, coming out of her warm bed. As she fully emerged, Aaron noticed an old collar on her neck. He moved her matted fur to see the collar closer. It was an old, tattered rope, loosely wrapped in an old bandana, cinched so tight it cut into a few spots of her skin and rubbed the fur off. He felt a knot well up in his throat as he carefully cut the makeshift collar off. Gurlz sat very still. Her big brown eyes stared right into his soul. Then, through eye contact, she seemed to thank him almost audibly. He went into the bathroom, got a washcloth, dampened it with warm water, and gently wiped her neck. She did cringe a bit at first touch, then relaxed and let him cleanse her wounds. She licked his hands when he finished, her way of showing gratitude.

Aaron put on his jacket and picked up the blanket.

“Let us go, my Gurlz,” he said, “We have a few stops to make, and I am starving.”

Gurlz got up and followed Aaron outside to the car. Aaron noticed that the cold and damp weather didn’t bother Gurlz, who waited for Aaron to put the blanket on the passenger seat before she jumped in. Then, Aaron drove down the street to the veterinary office.

Dr. Karl Stanley was an old-timer who had been the local vet long before Aaron was born. He was a sizeable gentleman, well over six feet tall, with a husky build. Always in jean overalls and a checkered lumberjack-style shirt, he looked a tad odd with his doctor’s lab coat and ever-present outback-style black leather hat. His ensemble was complete with a pair of black alligator leather combat boots. Dr. Stanley was a one-of-a-kind big, rough, and seemingly ageless-looking man, yet he had the most kind, gentle, and loving heart. All animals liked him without exception, Gurlz included. She got out of Aaron’s car and sat down at his feet.

After a complete examination, Dr. Stanley, whom the residents affectionately called "Stan, the Man," instructed Aaron on how to bring Gurlz back to optimum health. Due to being out alone in the woods for an undetermined amount of time, she was malnourished and would need to eat a healthy diet to normalize her weight. After he bathed and clipped her nails, he prescribed a topical ointment for her neck wounds. After all the pampering, she resembled a beautiful show dog, unrecognizable from earlier that morning.

Aaron thanked and paid Stan, the Man, for all his help. He purchased a pink camouflage walking harness and leash for Gurlz but decided not to get her a collar to allow her neck wounds a chance to heal without further irritation.

Since it was getting to be late afternoon, Aaron chose to walk Gurlz through the town. He gently put the harness on her. Gurlz patiently waited for him to open the car door, and then she jumped out. Aaron saw the local animal shelter off in the distance. His heart knew the dog would be in his life for a long time, but he knew it was best to stop there anyway to see if anyone inquired about Gurlz. He felt a flash of anger, remembering the signs of neglect on Gurlz.

Three

Evelyn Rose, Karl Stanley's sister, was in her late 60s. Forty years ago, she started the local animal shelter with her late husband, Joseph Rose. He had passed away almost twenty years ago, and she never remarried. However, both were very passionate about animal welfare, and Evelyn kept their dream alive.

She looked out her front picture window, her long grey hair twisted up into a bun, wisps of hair around her face. Evelyn constantly blew them out of her eyes. She was wise, people-smart, and followed her gut. She saw Aaron Peterik walking a dog toward the shelter and saw they had already formed a bond of friendship.

As Aaron approached the shelter, he worried. *What if someone was looking for Gurlz? Who had hurt her?* He looked up to catch a glimpse of Evelyn in the front window. She waved him to the side entrance of the building.

"Well, hello there, Aaron," she said. "And who is this lovely little lady with you?"

Gurlz sat beside Aaron and let Evelyn pet her affectionately on the head.

"This beautiful girl is my new friend. Since I picked her up this morning, I have been calling her "Gurlz." It seems she got herself left behind about ten kilometers out of town," Aaron explained.

"She sure is a pretty girl. Aren't you, my little sunshine?" Evelyn's hearty laugh was contagious, and Gurlz leaned in closer as Evelyn rubbed her behind the ears. Suddenly, Evelyn noticed the marks on Gurlz's neck.

"Has Karl seen her?" She peered at Aaron sternly.

Aaron explained what had happened that morning and about his trip to Karl's.

"You see, Evelyn, I have the space and the means to take care of her. My biggest concern is that someone will come looking for her. But with the wounds on her neck, I don't think it would be in her best interest to return."

Evelyn sighed as she blew her wispy hair out of her eyes. "Today seems to be your lucky day, Aaron. Fortunately for you, I do not have any kennels available right now. Besides, it will be a frosty day in July before *that* owner can have her back!"

"That is great news," Aaron said. " I do not expect anyone to come looking for her. But I will feel much better about that as time goes by."

He lovingly patted Gurlz and winked at her. Gurlz tilted her head to the right and closed her eyes. She could have sat there all day, basking in some much-needed kindness and love. Instead, she opened her eyes and looked at Aaron, thinking that if she could muster up tears, she would have cried for joy and said, "I love you, gentle human, Aaron." Her heart felt something good again, and she was coming alive on the inside.

Aaron and Gurlz visited with Evelyn for the rest of the afternoon. Evelyn cooked lunch for Aaron and got a big bowl of Blue Buffalo dog food and fresh water for Gurlz. As she watched Aaron share the last of his roast beef sandwich with Gurlz, she chuckled and said, "Try not to overdo it with the treats. She needs a well-balanced diet to get her back to 100%."

Both Aaron and Evelyn laughed. Gurlz looked at Aaron's empty plate, went to her food bowl, and ate everything. She then washed it down with lots of water. Since Aaron and Evelyn were chatting and having coffee, Gurlz went back beside Aaron and laid down. She put her head down on his feet and closed her eyes. Quickly she was asleep, dreaming of running and playing in a big grassy field, the gentle breeze in her fur and the sun's heat . . . wait, no, that wasn't the sun but the warmth of her new human's hands rubbing her belly and ribs. It tickled Gurlz, and she woke up enough to know that this beautiful feeling was not a dream. Instead, Aaron was gently stroking her fur.

"You are home now." Gurlz again heard that gentle whisper and went back to a peaceful sleep.

***

The rain had stopped, and the late afternoon sun was almost gone when Aaron and Gurlz walked back to the office. Gurlz practically pranced alongside Aaron as he carried an extra-large bag of dog food over his shoulder. Evelyn had convinced Aaron that Gurlz required only the best dog food available. She had also suggested that he should not give too her much human food, but they laughed as soon as the words came out of her mouth because Evelyn knew Gurlz would have an easy time putting on the necessary weight. She sensed there was not anything that Aaron would not do for Gurlz.

As Aaron and Gurlz arrived at Aaron's office, they heard a truck horn honking. He knew that sound well. It was the same car horn he remembered hearing as a child on a classic tv show. It had to be Stan, the Man! Aaron looked up and saw Karl and Evelyn waving at him as they drove by. He waved back and put the dog food into the trunk of his car. Aaron picked up the old blanket and went into his office with Gurlz to lock up for the night. He laid the blanket down again under his desk and did a quick clean-up while Gurlz laid down. Aaron turned off the lights and headed to the door.

As he reached to set the alarm, he noticed Gurlz was still on her blanket.

"Come on, Gurlz, time to go home," Aaron called out to Gurlz. There was no response. "Come along now, Gurlz," Aaron spoke a little louder but still did not get a response.

Slowly Aaron walked over to Gurlz. She was all curled up on her blanket in a deep sleep. Her long, terrifying ordeal had ended, and she was ready to *truly* rest because she felt safe with Aaron. So, Aaron gently bundled Gurlz up in her blanket and carried her to his car. She briefly opened her eyes as he put her onto the passenger seat. Aaron gently rubbed her head and said, "Everything will be okay now."

Gurlz closed her eyes and slept on the drive to Aaron's home.

As Aaron pulled up to his house, he gently nudged Gurlz awake from her peaceful slumber. She followed and shadowed his every move inside the house, through the kitchen, and onto the back deck. Aaron lit the BBQ and went back inside to get a steak. He returned with two ribeye steaks, one for him and one for Gurlz, and put them on the grill. Gurlz made herself comfortable beside the

BBQ and indulged her senses by occasionally inhaling the aroma of the ribeyes grilling to perfection.

After the steaks were ready, Aaron put one on a plate for Gurlz with a Blue Buffalo dog food side, and a caesar salad accompanied Aaron's steak. They ate their dinner together on the deck, and after a short relaxing spell, they played a good game of frisbee.

In the evenings, deer usually walked through Aaron's backyard on their way to the creek bordering his property. Aaron went inside to get water, and for the first time, he heard Gurlz bark. Her barks were playful and happy. Aaron looked out the window, and to his surprise, he saw Gurlz running around and playing with the deer.

He watched in disbelief, completely still, mesmerized by the activity. After a few moments, he shook his head and called for Gurlz to come back to the house. To his surprise, Gurlz ran right over to him, followed by the young deer! Gurlz abruptly stopped at Aaron's feet and turned to face the deer as if to introduce Aaron to her new friend. The young deer did not seem to fear Gurlz or Aaron and came nose to nose with Gurlz.

Even though Aaron could not believe what he saw, he did not make any sudden moves and enjoyed the interaction with the deer. Aaron sat on his back steps and watched Gurlz and the little deer run around and play tag. Gurlz would catch the deer and then run away, and amazingly, the deer would follow her before running away again for Gurlz to chase him. Finally, the young deer caught sight of his mom, nuzzled Gurlz, and ran into the night with her mom. As soon as the deer disappeared off into the woods, Gurlz ran to Aaron.

On any given evening, Aaron worked out in his home gym or went for a long run. But tonight was different. Aaron brushed his teeth, put on his pajamas, and climbed into bed. Gurlz jumped up into the bed and snuggled in next to Aaron. Then, the two drifted off into a deep, peaceful sleep.

Four

Aaron was in a deep sleep, dreaming he was on a towel at a white sand beach in a friendly, warm, and sunny climate. The waves gently rolled in. With every wave, a fine mist landed on Aaron's face. He smiled in his dream. Then the waves got bigger, and the water splashed directly onto his face. As the waves swelled, Aaron lifted his arms to try and shield his face from the water but felt dog fur. Immediately, he opened his eyes and found himself nose to nose with Gurlz. She was licking his face to wake him so she could go outside to do her morning business.

Aaron laughed and gave Gurlz a big hug.

"Good morning, my Gurlz," Aaron said as he wiped the dog slobber off his face. Gurlz jumped off the bed and ran to the door. She turned around, looked at Aaron, and barked. Aaron opened the door but kept a close watch to ensure she did not run too far from the house. But Gurlz stayed close to the house and came right back inside. The rain had restarted overnight, and Gurlz was not in the mood to get soaking wet again. She went to her food bowl and ate. But after a moment, she looked at Aaron. In her heart, she felt at peace with her newfound home and owner. Gurlz watched him go about in the kitchen making his breakfast. That was when Aaron caught a glimpse of Gurlz watching him, smiled, and tossed her a piece of his omelet. She caught it mid-toss and swallowed. Gurlz then took a long drink of her water and went over to lay down at Aaron's feet. He sat at the kitchen table eating the rest of his omelet and enjoying a cup of freshly brewed coffee.

Today was Saturday, so Aaron was not going into his office but handled business from home. After eating, he cleaned his kitchen as Gurlz remained in her spot. She was content to rest there, snoozing and watching this human Aaron go about his weekend routine. Aaron noticed Gurlz watching him.

The broom reminded Gurlz of when a man shook a broom handle at her. She could not fully remember that person but knew that Aaron was different. He was gentle and kind to her, and when he looked at her, he saw *her*. She knew already that she had seen the honest Aaron—a human man who would never harm her, which solidified the good feelings she had for him. She felt alive, and a peaceful calm filled her inside. She put her head down on top of her paws and smiled. Gurlz knew he would not know she was smiling, so she winked at him. The trust and love she had heard about were absolute.

"What are you looking at, my Gurlz?" Aaron chuckled. "If I did not know any better, I would think you were smiling at me."

He walked across the kitchen and patted Gurlz on the forehead. Then he knelt and gently checked her neck. Her wounds did look a smidge better. He applied more of the medicated ointment; Gurlz sat very still for Aaron. She felt wonderfully blessed to have someone take the time for her. She could not resist the urge to thank Aaron and turned to him and licked his hands and face. Aaron laughed and wiped his face with his sleeve.

"Love you, too, Gurlz," he said and got up.

Aaron looked out the window and saw the rain was still coming down, and the clouds were a dark gray. The sun had no chance of penetrating through the cloud coverage. It certainly was not a day to venture too far outside, except for a long run in the rain. Aaron loved to run in the rain because the cool water felt perfect during those times. Although Aaron did not run professionally, he was a strong, fast runner.

Because of what Gurlz had gone through, Aaron decided to leave her at home. He would only be gone for an hour, so she could roam free in the house until he got back. He put on his running gear and filled Gurlz's water and food bowls.

"Be good, my Gurlz. I will not be gone too long," Aaron said, "I promise."

Aaron ran down the long driveway and the long winding gravel road. The rain fell quickly, and the water droplets were cold on his skin. He thought of Gurlz and smiled and picked up his pace as he pictured her looking out the window, waiting for him.

***

Back at Aaron's house, Gurlz was not happy. Thoughts that she was again abandoned rolled through her mind. She tried to find a way out of the house, but nothing opened for her. Finally, she jumped up against the front door, where she saw Aaron running away from the house, but Gurlz could not get out the door. Her heart raced as her fear turned into panic. She ran through the house, looking for a way out. As she passed each window, Aaron got smaller as he got farther away until finally, he was gone.

Gurlz's heart felt heavy and sank fast into the pit of her stomach. She made her way into the ensuite bathroom in Aaron's bedroom. The window above the vanity mirror was slightly open. Gurlz jumped onto the sink and leaped through the window without hesitation. Amazingly, the window did not break and opened enough for Gurlz to get out.

Unknown to Gurlz, there was a ten-foot drop to the ground from the window. She nearly missed a large stone planter positioned under the window, landed on the wet grass and slid to a stop. Aaron was nowhere in sight, and to add to her grief, the rain started to pour. Since she did not know exactly where she was, she did not want to repeat another lonely, scary adventure in a rainstorm. Gurlz went over to the deck and did her best to stay dry. The deck had a lattice around the bottom, so she went under the steps.

Gurlz was confused about why she was alone again, but when she saw his car was still there, she decided to wait, hoping he could not have gone too far. Thunder rolled loudly, and a bolt of lightning flashed wildly across the sky. Gurlz felt afraid and blinked her eyes twice. She was sure her imagination was not playing tricks on her when she saw Aaron run toward the house. He was drenched from rain and sweat and hurried to get out of the thunder and lightning and home, where he knew Gurlz would require his companionship.

Aaron was surprised to see Gurlz come out from under the steps and run toward him. Wondering how she managed to get outside, he caught Gurlz in the air as she jumped right up into his arms.

"Hey, my little Houdini," Aaron said and laughed.

He carried his Gurlz inside the house, wrapped her in a bath towel, and dried her off as best he could, but then she shook the rest of the water off. Aaron looked at the water spots on the wall and the wet footprints across the floor.

"Well, now, my Gurlz," he said, "it looks like I will be doing a bit more cleaning today. But do not worry about anything; you are safe and dry now."

He looked up at the bathroom window and shook his head in disbelief.

"You could have landed on that planter, you silly girl. No more jumping out windows," Aaron said.

Gurlz leaned against him, and Aaron patted her wet head. He was not at all upset with Gurlz and was so thankful she had not gotten hurt. Gurlz was very happy that her human was back.

***

Aaron and Gurlz spent the next few hours at home. Later, he showered and dressed in his weekend clothes—a faded pair of jeans, a Christian rock band t-shirt, topped off with a black leather jacket. Next, he picked up his car keys and pushed the remote start. Gurlz heard the car start and got up. She headed straight for the front door and waited for Aaron, who laughed aloud when he saw her. "Yes, Gurlz, you are coming with me into town. I need to get more groceries for us."

He put on his favourite pair of combat boots and opened the door for Gurlz. They both ran through the rain to the car. The storm had not stopped, and now and then, thunder and lightning blasted across the sky. Gurlz did not seem bothered by the bad weather today, but she stayed very close to Aaron. The two settled into the PT Cruiser for the ride to town.

Aaron turned on the radio to the local station just in time for the news update and was thrilled to hear no news about anyone looking for a lost dog. Unfortunately, however, the weather report called for thunderstorms all weekend.

Aaron reached over and rested his hand on Gurlz's shoulders. She was stretched out across the passenger seat, not quite asleep, her head now closer to Aaron.

When they drove past where Aaron had first seen Gurlz, he looked over at her, but she had fallen fast asleep and looked peaceful and happy, a completely different dog from yesterday morning.

As Aaron turned off the highway onto Snail Street, the main street in the small town of Victory, Gurlz still slept peacefully.

Passenger seat? He thought, *more like Gurlz's seat.*

Aaron pulled into the grocery store parking lot and smiled lovingly at Gurlz. He knew not to leave her in the car alone but could not take her inside the grocery store. *Okay, think, Aaron. How do I handle this?* At that moment, he saw Evelyn Rose walking out of the store with a loaf of bread and waved. She waved back and walked over to his car.

Meanwhile, Gurlz felt the car stop and opened her eyes to see Aaron open his car window to say hello to Evelyn. Gurlz recognized Evelyn's voice as the friendly lady who had helped her out yesterday. She sat up and wagged her tail.

"Good morning, Aaron," said Evelyn, "and how is Gurlz doing today?"

"Good morning, Evelyn," Aaron replied. "Gurlz is fine today, but she needs a little company while I go into the store."

Evelyn listened to Aaron tell her about Gurlz's big adventure that morning. Then, when he finished, she offered to sit with Gurlz until he finished his grocery shopping. Fortunately, it had stopped raining.

The grocery store was right beside the coffee shop Aaron visited every morning, so before he went into the grocery store, he got Evelyn a coffee and a plain donut for Gurlz. Evelyn and Gurlz had moved from the car to the bench beside the grocery store. He gave Evelyn her coffee and Gurlz her donut. Aaron patted Gurlz and told her to be good for Evelyn. And Gurlz obeyed Aaron and stayed with Evelyn the whole time he was gone.

Five

Aaron made quick time in the grocery store. He got everything he needed, plus a few more treats for Gurlz. After paying, he found Gurlz still beside Evelyn. She felt comfortable with Evelyn but wondered where Aaron had gone. His car was still there so she was sure he would return soon.

And as soon as Aaron emerged from the store pushing his grocery cart, Gurlz stood up and whined. She poked at Evelyn with her front paw, who could not help but laugh. Gurlz looked so cute and happy when she saw Aaron.

"Go on, Gurlz. Go meet him," Evelyn said and laughed as Gurlz jumped off the bench and ran toward Aaron. When Aaron saw Gurlz jump off the bench and run toward him, he remembered how she had jumped into his arms earlier and instinctively moved from behind the shopping cart. Evelyn could not believe her eyes. She sat in awe as the dog ran to her human and jumped into his arms.

Gurlz made her final leap, and Aaron braced himself and caught her mid-flight. He gave her a big hug and gently put her down. Gurlz proudly walked beside him as he pushed his grocery cart to the PT Cruiser. Evelyn joined them by the car. Aaron and Evelyn engaged in a small chat while he loaded the groceries into the car. He returned the cart, thanked Evelyn for her help, and gave her a ride to her animal shelter.

On the drive, Aaron asked if anyone had come looking for Gurlz. Evelyn reassured him that no one had inquired about a lost female dog in the area, and in fact, Evelyn had also done some investigating of her own earlier that morning. She was quite happy to inform Aaron know that no one had been looking for a lost dog. Although she had made a few inquiring phone calls to locate the previous owner, she was not sad when she had no luck. As owner of an animal shelter, Evelyn was still bewildered by the number of dogs left roaming around or dropped off and never reclaimed.

Aaron and Gurlz thanked Evelyn for all her help and drove toward Aaron's office because he remembered that he had to pick up a file. As they pulled up to the front of his office, a large muscular man of Native Canadian ancestry stood at the front door. He wore a long black duster-style jacket over a t-shirt and a pair of jeans. But he also wore cowboy boots and a cowboy hat. His long black hair was pulled back into a simple ponytail, and next to him was a black SUV.

Aaron sighed heavily and put the car into park. When he had inherited a small sum from his parents at eighteen and used the funds to start his own business, despite his success, he never liked to have to collect on unpaid bonds. That is where Matt Bear came into the picture. Matt was a bounty hunter by trade and the sensei of a private training camp for self-defence. He was also Aaron's sensei.

"Okay, Gurlz. You can wait here for me. I will not be too long," Aaron said. He put the front windows down an inch to give Gurlz fresh air while he went inside.

Gurlz sat in the driver's seat and watched Aaron go into his office with Matt. Even though she had never met this human, she felt no reason to fear him. Instead, she watched as they talked. Aaron reached into his filing cabinet and gave Matt some files. They chatted for a few more minutes and then shook hands. Matt smiled as he walked by the car and said to Gurlz, "Hello there, you pretty girl. Take care of that guy."

He motioned towards the office. "He takes care of many people."

Gurlz barked happily in response. It was an "I agree with you," kind of bark. She looked at him and wagged her tail. Matt laughed waved goodbye. Aaron chuckled and waved back. He had watched the encounter between Matt and Gurlz and was not surprised to see her so welcoming. It was apparent that Gurlz had sensed the good in Matt, which made Aaron happy.

Aaron set the security alarm and exited his office. Gurlz hopped over to the passenger seat when he approached his car. Then, he got into the car and drove off towards home.

Six

As the weeks passed, Gurlz grew more comfortable with Aaron, her anxiety almost gone. Whenever Aaron had to be without Gurlz, he had Evelyn dogsit. When Aaron went to his office every day, he got up an hour earlier so that he and Gurlz could go for a morning run. Then Gurlz usually spent the day with Aaron at work, and on some occasions, she spent a few hours with Evelyn at the kennel.

Aaron had organized his office better to accommodate Gurlz. He had gotten her a sizeable pink camo and comfy dog bed tucked under his big desk. Beside his desk were two metal dog feeding bowls. One was pink for her food, and the other was purple for her water.

Gurlz was a welcome addition to Aaron's office. All of Aaron's clients enjoyed her company, and she was very friendly with anyone Aaron welcomed into his business. Whenever someone entered the front door, a bell rang, and Gurlz would bark just once, then sit beside Aaron's chair.

It was not long before Aaron's clients brought treats for Gurlz on their visits. Some even stopped only to bring Gurlz a treat and say hello. In fact, after a few months, Aaron's business had increased by fifteen percent. When someone asked Aaron where he got Gurlz, he told them the story but never said that he rescued Gurlz; he said they found each other through God's grace. Aaron also encouraged anyone wanting to help animals to see Evelyn at the kennel. She was able to help find five dogs a new home so far through Aaron's suggestion. In the kennel, Evelyn hung posters for Aaron's bail bond business, featuring a picture of Gurlz. Likewise, Aaron put up posters for Evelyn's kennel in his establishment. Both businesses were reaping the rewards, so Stan, the Man, also featured his business at Evelyn's and Aaron's and vice versa. It was not very long before he saw the benefits as well. Evelyn, Stan, the Man, Aaron, and a few other local businesses also chose to pool together some finances and put up two giant, brightly lit billboards at either end of town. This advertising was perfect for the businesses within Victory. It drew in many more customers from the nearby highways. Unfortunately, along with the good thing also came the bad.

Aaron was experiencing an upswing in business. He had hired Carol to clean the office every other day to accommodate his busier schedule. Though she was still working at the coffee shop, she took on a few jobs cleaning offices to save money for her retirement. In addition, Aaron had a bell that chimed loudly when the front door opened. Since the town of Victory's location is in a valley, the wind sometimes fiercely blasted through the downtown core. The constant chiming agitated Carol, so she pushed the bell up so it would not catch the wind. Usually, she remembered to put the bell back in place.

Unfortunately, she had cleaned Aaron's office the previous night and forgot to put the bell back. Unknown to Carol, a professional thief watched her moves to find out which businesses to target. He planned to come back on a night when Carol was not cleaning. He saw her mistake and intended to rob Aaron's office the next night. He already had other places lined up for tonight.

"Like taking candy from a baby," he snarled and laughed aloud. Then he drove off towards his first victim's business.

Seven

Aaron was working late at the office. He had to bring his car into the shop that afternoon for an oil change, tire rotation, and alignment. He planned to walk to the shop and pick up his car when he finished work. Gurlz was enjoying an early evening nap on her bed under the desk. The evening air was warm and humid, and the setting sun was still enough light for Aaron not to have to turn on the lights. He went into the bathroom at the back of the office.

From the outside, the building looked empty. The sun reflected an image of an unoccupied parking lot off the large front tinted windows. The thief smiled as he quietly pulled up alongside the building. He remembered that the bell was not in place and planned on a quick, easy break-in and enter. He was also pleasantly surprised to find the front door unlocked as well.

Gurlz was used to hearing footsteps outside the building. She was always ready to see who was there when the bell chimed or to see the next treat delivery. Tonight the door opened, but the bell did not chime. Instinctively, she knew something was amiss. Aaron came out of the bathroom, which surprised the thief, who fumbled while attempting to retrieve his gun. Gurlz took quick advantage and sprang into action by leaping out from under the desk and jumping at the intruder. She flew through the air, putting her body directly in front of Aaron. The gunshot hit her in the side. Gurlz provided the moment that Aaron needed to disarm the gunman. He grabbed the first thing he could, a solid heavy coffee mug, and threw it at the assailant, hitting the gun and knocking it out of his hand. Due to his martial arts training, Aaron had no problem subduing the thief. Then he immediately rushed to Gurlz's side. She was on the floor, bleeding from her right side. Gurlz slightly raised her head, briefly focused her eyes on Aaron, and then passed out.

When she awoke, she was in her big comfy bed at home and felt Aaron's soft touch as he pet her gently. She heard the birds singing outside and the breeze rustling the leaves in the nearby trees. Gurlz was happy to be safe at home. Her side hurt when she tried to move, but she had been very fortunate that the bullet had gone through her body and *miraculously, it passed by all her major organs.* Stan, the Man, had given her a diagnosis: a full recovery, and she did! Aaron and Gurlz continued to live in the small town of Victory and spent a lot of time at Matt's place helping Gurlz heal.

Matt had a pet of his own. He had previously adopted a Rottweiler from Evelyn, raised him from a pup, and named him Tony. During their time together, Gurlz and Tony eventually had a small litter of puppies, for which Evelyn was able to find loving homes. Aaron and Gurlz kept one of them and named her Hazel. Gurlz knew that she would not be leaving him alone when she left this life because she taught Hazel how to take care of Aaron. Gurlz found out that love is a special bond between two different life forms: a man and his dog.

Hebrews 13:1-2

Keep on loving each other as brothers and sisters. Don't forget to show hospitality to strangers, for some who have done this have entertained angels without realizing it.

www.ingramcontent.com/pod-product-compliance
Lightning Source LLC
Chambersburg PA
CBHW070619310726
48982CB00001B/122

* 9 7 8 1 7 7 8 2 4 4 1 0 0 *